That's What Leprechauns Do

by Eve Bunting
Illustrated by Emily Arnold McCully

Clarion Books
New York

Clarion Books
a Houghton Mifflin Company imprint
215 Park Avenue South, New York, NY 10003
Text copyright © 2005 by Edward D. Bunting and Anne E. Bunting Family Trust
Illustrations copyright © 2005 by Emily Arnold McCully

The illustrations were executed in watercolor.
The text was set in 14-point OPTI Adrift.

www.houghtonmifflinbooks.com

Printed in the U.S.A.

Library of Congress Cataloging-in-Publication Data
Bunting, Eve, 1928—
That's what leprechauns do / by Eve Bunting :
illustrated by Emily Arnold McCully.
p. cm.
Summary: When leprechauns Ari, Boo, and Col need to place the pot of gold
at the end of the rainbow, they cannot help getting into mischief along the way.
ISBN 0-618-35410-7
[1. Leprechauns—Fiction.] I. Title: That's what leprechauns do.
II. McCully, Emily Arnold, ill. III. Title.
PZ7.B91527Th 2005
[E]—dc22   2004022941

ISBN-13: 978-0-618-35410-8
ISBN-10: 0-618-35410-7

WOZ 10 9 8 7 6 5 4 3 2

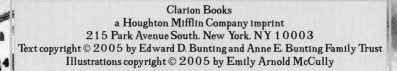

To my friends the Maghera Leprechauns
—E.B.

For Claire and Maya
—E.A.M.

The three leprechauns sat under the chestnut tree.
Ari looked up at the cloud-filled sky. "It's coming," he said.
"And there's work to be done."

Boo and Col put on their red shoes and their caps, and strapped their packs to their backs.

"We're ready," Boo said. "But why is it always us that has to put the pot of gold at the end of the rainbow?"

"Especially since not a single soul ever finds it," Col added.

Ari looked from one of them to the other. "Don't be asking," he said. "It's leprechaun duty, so it is. And fellows! Remember! It's coming, so there'll be no time for mischief along the way."

They walked in line, the one in front of the other, the other one behind.

"No mischief, no mischief along the way," they chanted.

But when they got to Ballybunion Farm, they saw
Mrs. Ballybunion's cow, Pansy, standing in the field.
Ari whipped out the little bottle of red paint he kept in his
backpack for leprechaun business. He ran across to Pansy.
"Stand still, my lovely," he told her, and he painted her
hooves scarlet red.

Pansy looked down. "Pretty!" she said.

"Imagine Mrs. Ballybunion's face when she comes to milk you!"
Ari shouted. He and Boo and Col rolled over and over in the grass,
laughing.

"She'll think I've been to a dance." Pansy did a couple of small hop-and-steps to demonstrate.

The leprechauns clapped and whistled. "We'd be delighted to join you in a waltz or two," Ari exclaimed. "But we're in a desperate hurry."

"I thought there was to be no mischief along the way," Boo reminded him.

"Och, sure, but I couldn't help myself. Mischief's what leprechauns do," Ari said. "Along with our more important duties." He glanced up at the tatters of clouds in the sky. "And we'd better not delay, for we've delayed enough already."

But as they were passing Old Jamie Bradley's house, they saw Jamie's gray woolen long johns spread out to dry on his hawthorn hedge.

The leprechauns looked at each other and grinned. Quick as a cat pounce, they ran across to the hedge and stood one on top of the other and the other on top of him. Ari reached up and tied the two long-john legs together in a tight knot.

They almost fell off each other, they laughed so hard.

"It would be great altogether to stay and watch Old Jamie try putting his legs into those," Boo said. "But it will be a month of Sundays before they're dry, and we've no time to waste."

They took a few minutes to somersault across Liam McGabe's garden. There was a yellow tennis ball in the middle of the road, and they rolled it along with them as they went.

Miss Maud Murphy's hen, Bridie, clucked at them from behind her gate.

"Bridie!" Ari said. "Would you be doing us a favor? Could we trundle this ball up to your nest, and could you sit on it for us? It'll be the great joke on Miss Maud Murphy when she comes out to gather your eggs."

Bridie put her head to one side. "It's not going to be easy sitting on that. But the three of you were so good to me, scaring that fox away from my henhouse last night. I'll do it."

Col stretched up and patted her wing. "Thank you, Bridie."

They squeezed themselves through the gate and tumbled the ball with them. Then they heaved it up and into Bridie's nest. She gave a trial sit on it.

"I'll be sore underneath myself for a week," she grumbled. "But the thought of Miss Maud Murphy's face when she sees I've laid a yellow ball will be worth it."

"Won't that beat all," Col gasped.

"The three of you can't help making mischief, can you?" Bridie asked.

"That's what leprechauns do," Ari told her. "Along with our more important duties." He stopped. "Is that a spitting of wet I feel?"

"'Tis." Boo stared up at the sky, where the sun was flickering through heavy clouds. A thin cool rain had started to fall.

"Hurry! Hurry!" Ari ordered. "It's come! We can't be late!"

They pulled their green slickers from their backpacks and settled their caps low to their ears.

Anybody seeing them racing along the road would have taken them for three green leaves. But they were leprechauns, and they had work to do.

"Get them out, boyos, get them ready," Ari said. They took their little spades from their backpacks. Then they stopped for a minute to look up at the rainbow, blue and green and yellow and pink, that was arched across half the sky.

"There it is," Ari said with satisfaction. "Come on!"

They dashed across Padddywhackers Bog, found the place there where they kept the pot of gold buried for just such a rainbow occasion, and dug it up.

Ari stood in the middle of the bog. "Here," he said. The three of them placed the pot of glittering gold in just the right spot and watched the rainbow curve itself all the way down till it ended on top of the pot.

The leprechauns settled themselves to wait. They tootled some grass-stalk music, threw raindrops at each other, and ate the rosehips they'd brought for snacks.

They waited long. But nobody came.

Once again, nobody came.

"You'd think *somebody* would find it," Col complained.

"Somebody will. Someday," Ari said.

"Maybe we should put up a sign," Boo suggested. "'Pot of gold, this way.'"

"No, no!" Ari said. "That's not how it's done. There's a bit of magic to the finding, and a bit of luck, and a bit of imagination, too. That gold's waiting for just the right person."

The rain had stopped. The sun went behind a cloud. The rainbow shortened itself, then disappeared.

"No use waiting any longer." Col took off his cap and wrung the wet out of it. "If we hurry, we could be in time to see Miss Maud Murphy discover Bridie's big yellow egg," he said.

Boo laughed. "Won't that be the great thing to see!"

"All right, then," Ari said. "We'll put a rush on this."

They buried the pot again in its usual place.

Ari patted the smoothed-down bog dirt. "Don't worry, Pot," he whispered. "We'll be back to get you on the next rainbow day. Now we're off again to see what new mischief we can find. For besides our important duties, that's what leprechauns do!"

About Leprechauns

According to legend, the leprechaun is a tiny elf, found only in Ireland. Most leprechauns are shoemakers to the fairies, who pay them gold for their work. The leprechauns, or "little people," store their gold in pots and often bury one "at the end of a rainbow." Since leprechauns love more than anything to play tricks, this may just be another one. The gold at the end of the rainbow has not been discovered yet! But if you find a leprechaun and pick him up, he must tell you where his gold is hidden. That is leprechaun law.

So look for leprechauns in Ireland near clear springs of water, or close to large rock formations, or at the end of a rainbow. Listen for the sound of tiny hammers tapping, or elfin pipes piping, as small voices sing a fairy song. And maybe, just maybe, you will find the leprechauns' pot of gold!